Fuddle, The Monster of Confusion

The Monster Who Couldn't Decide

a WorryWoo Tale

by Andi Green

ISBN 978-0-9792860-3-2
Printed in China

E
GRE

To see all The WorryWoo Monsters™
go to www.WorryWoos.com

This book is dedicated to Shelby
whose image is reflected in all
of my characters.

In a bustling town in the land of WorryWoos,

a monster named Fuddle
always felt so confused.

With so many stores and so many signs,
she could never decide or make up her mind.

If she needed a hat, she would get in a tizzy,
there were so many choices she'd always feel dizzy.

"I want this one...

no that one,"

she'd firmly declare,

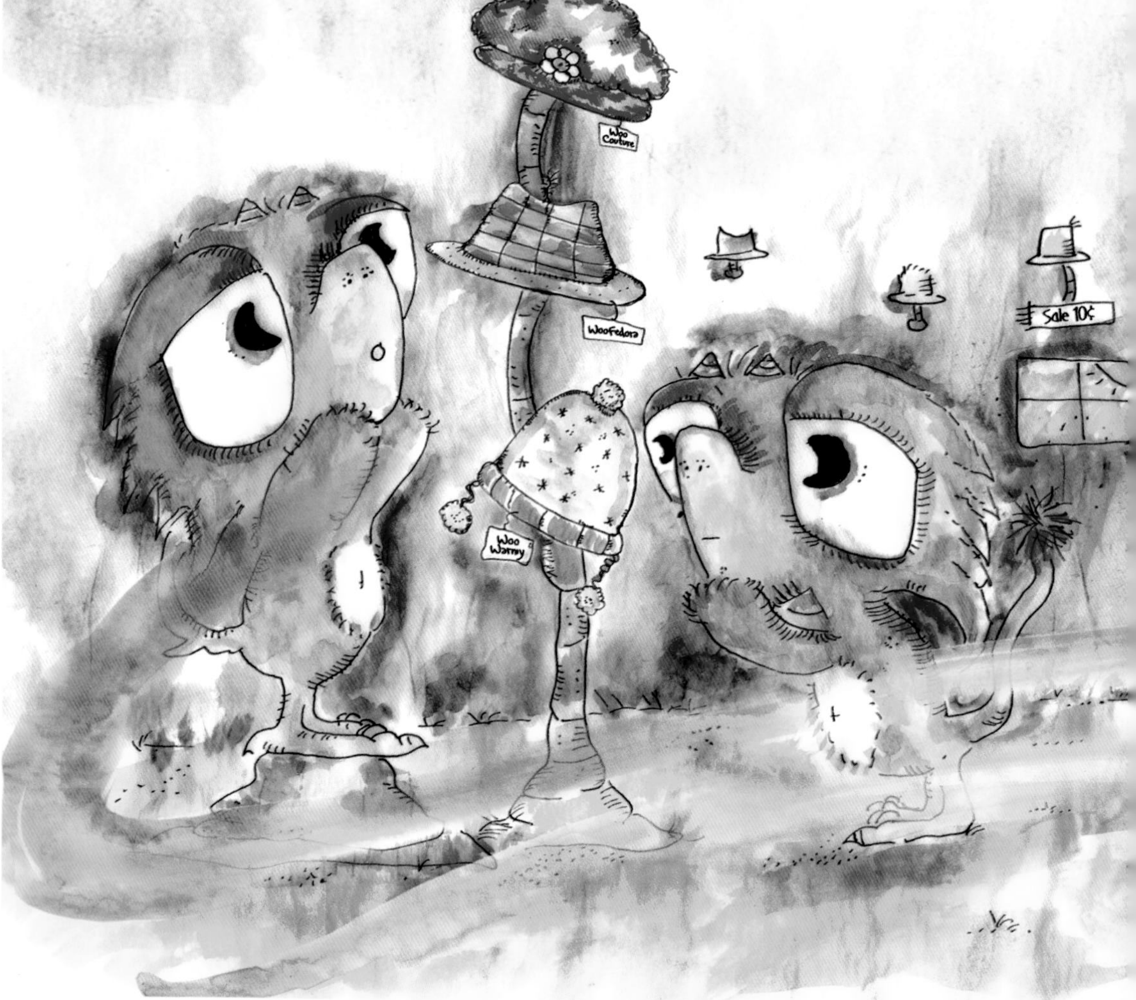

as she searched all around for the RIGHT one to wear.

But the styles and patterns and pom poms
to match, made Fuddle cry out,

"I don't want a new hat!"

Then her tummy would rumble
and she'd feel so upset,

'cause she just couldn't
pick what she thought was

the BEST!

Befuddled and sad she
would head for the door,

though where she was going - she just wasn't sure.

"I think I'd like a muffin,"
she'd say with a smile.

seeing pancakes and waffles and fruit cups with whip,

blueberry yogurt and veggies with dip!

"They even have **tacos...**

...oh look, rhubarb pie!"

Her heart would start

pounding

as she'd stare in surprise.

"Oh, I don't want to eat,"
she'd exclaim and then go.

"I think I would rather go out and play;

Hmmm...

who should I call on this beautiful day?"

Wince

Rue

Twitch

Squeek

Nola

"We could jump rope or fly kites or maybe agree
to visit the museum, there is so much to see."

But **bigger** and
bigger
the choice would become,

'til all of her options didn't seem like much fun.

Then she'd say to herself,

"I don't want to play,"

and have nothing to do except go on her way.

So, the story would end the same every time,

since Fuddle could **never** make up her mind.

She kept running in circles
wondering what she should do,

trying to decide, but not having a clue.

When **suddenly** she saw
a site to behold,

signs hanging from flowers
with colors quite bold.

Scratching her head asking,

"What can this be?"

Fuddle heard from the ground a soft melody.

And there she did spot wiggling along,

a silly little worm
singing a song.

He was wearing a wool cap all fuzzy and blue,
munching on mud cakes with grass covered goo.

You could hear him belt out between

giant slurps,

Then, he squiggled around and stopped at her feet.

"Welcome to my garden. I come here all the time,

to sit and to think

"You see, sometimes I'm frightened
and sometimes I feel...

that the **smallest** of choices is such a big deal."

...so I simply *decide*."

Fuddle listened intently, as a new day did rise,
and looked at the worm with **wide** misty eyes.

"But if you choose wrong,
what happens next?"

She wiped back a tear for she felt so perplexed.

"Oh dear," said the worm,
"there's no reason to cry."

"Believe in yourself;
you really must try."

"Every day's an adventure and
with each choice you make,

you'll learn
something NEW
with each step
that you take."

"You'll only miss out—
if you don't choose at all."

"Well, I did want a muffin,"
Fuddle said with a smile.

"And a hat would be nice;
      I can pick ANY style!"

"That's right," said her new friend,
"and when you are done...

...you'll find making decisions can be so much fun!"

Fading into the flowers away he did squirm.

Fuddle was happy she had met Mr. Worm!

Now, when she's confused,
as she may feel at times,

she remembers his garden...

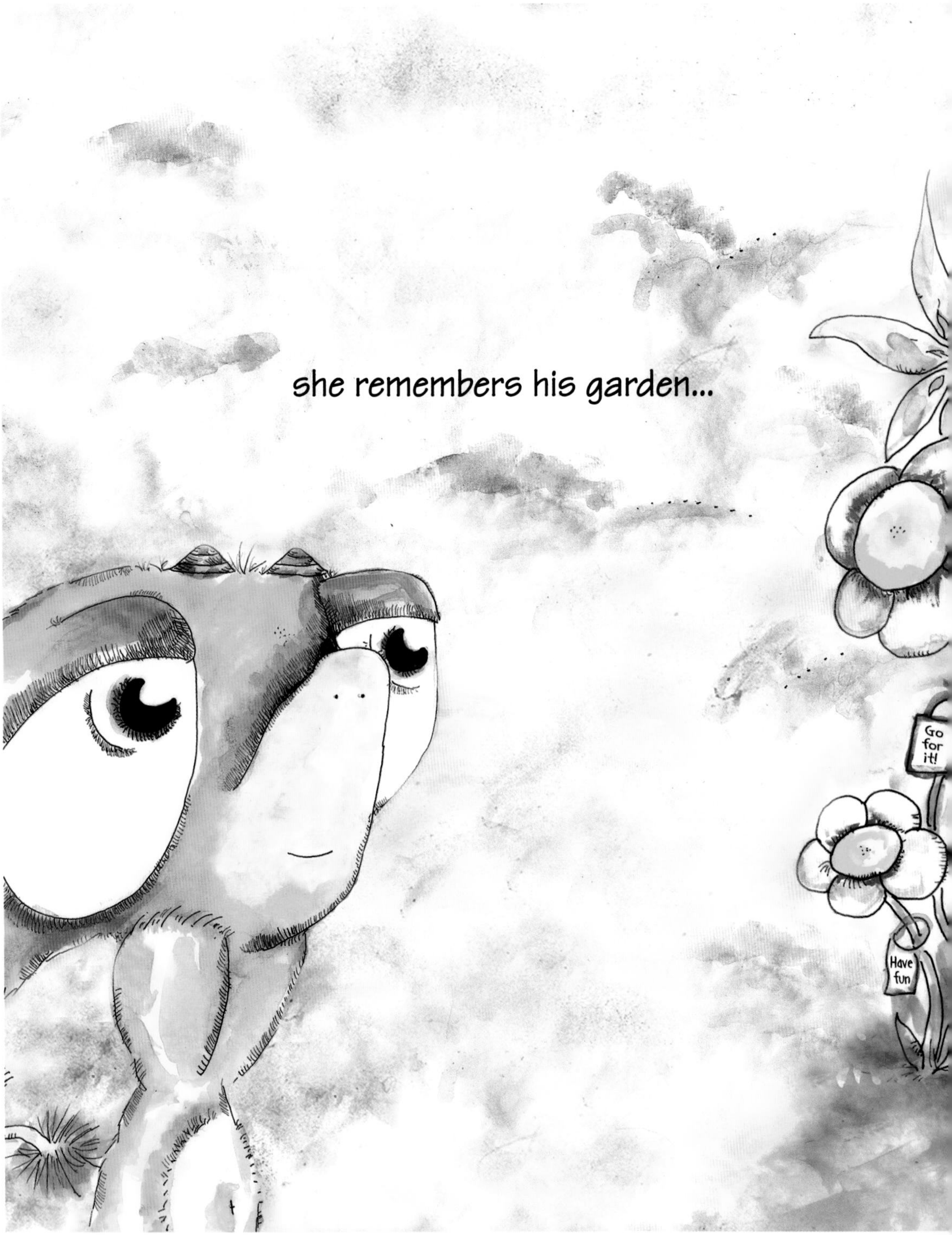

and the words on the signs.

And all of her doubts just drift away,

'cause she knows with each choice

...it will all be OK!

About the Author:

Andi Green is a bird-loving, cat-cuddling, dog-snuggling monster-maker who started her career as an Art Director in NYC. She is currently the writer and illustrator of The WorryWoo Monsters series. Accolades of her work include: a Silver Moonbeam Children's Book Award, a Creative Child Magazine Award, and an iParenting Media Award. Her work has also been featured on the Today Show. Andi's goal is to help children embrace their emotions and find their inner Woo.

Other books by Andi Green include:

- The Lonely Little Monster
- The Nose That Didn't Fit
- The Monster in The Bubble